SAGE
COOKSON'S
Sweet Escape

SALLY MURPHY

SAGE
COOKSON'S

Sweet
Escape

For my family,

who love chocolate as much as I do.

First published in the UK in 2020
by New Frontier Publishing Europe Ltd
Uncommon, 126 New King's Road, London, SW6 4LZ
www.newfrontierpublishing.co.uk
ISBN: 978-1-912858-65-1

Cover illustration and design by Celeste Hulme

Printed and bound in China

1 3 5 7 9 10 8 6 4 2

CHAPTER 1

'Bye Sage! Don't forget me, will you?'

'As if!' My friend Lucy is so totally not the kind of friend you could forget. Even if you wanted to, which I don't.

We've been friends since we met in the book corner on the first day of kindy. Back then we connected because we both loved the same book: *Are You My Mother?* by Dr Seuss. Now we still love reading the same books, but we also love lots of other things:

shopping, movies, rollerskating along the river near our houses, animals – just about everything, in fact. We have so much in common.

'And bring me back something yummy!' Lucy calls after me, her dark hair bobbing.

'Will see what I can manage,' I reply as I open the door of Mum's car, which has just pulled into the school pick-up bay.

That's another reason Lucy and I are such good friends. She's happy for me that I get to travel and see such interesting places. Some of the kids at school seem a bit jealous when I come back talking about the places I've seen. Others think it's weird how I miss so much school. But Lucy just accepts it as part of who I am.

'Have a brilliant time!' she calls after me. I wave out the window as Mum pulls away from the kerb, carefully guiding her little black sports car into the traffic.

I think Lucy actually likes having a friend who travels so much. I share my adventures with her as much as I can.

While I'm away we exchange emails, and chat on the phone nearly every day. And on this trip, for the first time, we will be able to keep in touch via text message. At last our parents have agreed that we can have mobile phones to stay in contact.

'So long as you don't overdo it.' That was what my dad said.

'And no texts during school hours or after bedtime.' That was what Lucy's mum said.

'Yippee!' was what Lucy and I both said, hugging each other excitedly.

So saying goodbye to Lucy this time around hasn't been quite as hard as usual.

CHAPTER 2

'**D**ad's going to meet us at the airport,' says Mum.

'Okay,' I say. I don't ask if he's remembered my suitcase, because I'm sure that he has. If he hasn't remembered it, Mum or one of their assistants will have organised everything. When you travel as much as we do, you have to be organised.

Why do we travel so much? Because we're 'The Cooksons'. Well, Mum and Dad are, anyway. They are famous television cooks and gastronomes (a fancy way of saying they are food experts). And when your parents have a cooking show as successful as *The Cooksons Cook On*, travelling is something you get used to.

Mum and Dad explore the country, and sometimes the world, learning about the food of different regions. Then they make episodes of their show about what they find.

The fun part is: they take me with them. Wherever they go, I go too. So while they are busy making their show, I am busy visiting cool places. Don't get too excited, though: unless it's school holidays, I also have to go to school in those cool places, or work on my schoolwork with a tutor.

Right now we are heading west for a couple of weeks. I take one last look back at Lucy, still waiting in the school car park for her mum to collect her.

'Don't worry,' Mum's voice comes from the front of the car. 'It's only a week apart.'

'I know.' I hold up my mobile phone. 'And this time we'll be able to text.'

Right on cue, my phone buzzes.

Have fun.

Watch out for rogue frogs. x

I laugh out loud. Only Lucy knows how scared I am of frogs. She always teases me, but only when there are no frogs around. I quickly text back.

I'm going to catch one and bring it back for you. Then we'll see who's scared! Xx

CHAPTER 3

The next day I wake up in my room at Newhaven Resort, deep in the South West of Western Australia. Mum, who has come in to see if I'm awake, opens the long red curtains that cover the window.

'Good morning sleepyhead,' she says, coming to sit on the edge of my bed.

'Good morn– oh!' I can't talk for a minute. The view from my bedroom window is too amazing for words. It had been dark and very late when we'd arrived last night after a long flight and an even longer drive.

'Stunning, isn't it?' asks Mum.

I climb out of bed and together we stand at the window, taking in the view.

There's a swimming pool just a couple of metres away from my bed, which by itself would be pretty amazing, but past that the scene is even more spectacular.

The pool goes right to the edge of some sort of drop. Below, a rolling green valley gives way to lush green forest. Wispy steam rises gently from the surface of the pool, suggesting that it is heated, but even then I'm not sure it is warm enough to swim in right now.

'Wow!' I say. 'Sure beats a hotel in a busy city.'

'Too right!' says Mum.

It's all lovely to look at, but I realise that

I haven't even asked why we're here in Newhaven at all. What foods could be grown here? We always go places where there's something delicious growing or being made.

Maybe Mum can read my mind, because right on cue she lets me in on her plans. 'Dad and I are off to see a man about some chocolate.' She watches my face. My smile must be the reaction she's looking for. 'So you want to come then?'

'Chocolate?' Only my favourite food in the whole world. 'Of course! Have I got time for a shower?' Already I'm across the room opening my suitcase, looking for something to wear.

Mum laughs. 'Slow down. You've got plenty of time.' She hands me a pair of socks that have dropped from my suitcase. 'Breakfast first, and Dad and I will need to chat with Dave and Sheila.' Dave and Sheila are from the film crew that travel with us. 'You've got about an hour. When you're dressed, come next door and we'll have breakfast.'

I take a deep breath. Phew. I'm still a bit tired from our flight last night, and the long drive from the airport in the hire car.

I take my phone from the charger.

Made it safely. Hotel has an amazing view.

As I sort out my clothes ready for the shower, my phone chimes with a reply.

Cool. Miss you already. What you doing today? I've got netball.

I reply quickly.

Hope you win! I'm going to meet a chocolatier ☺ Better go. Talk soon x

I push open the door into my bathroom. The thought of a day in a chocolate factory helps me get ready quickly.

CHAPTER 4

We are surprised to see a *Closed* sign at the front of Marco's Chocolates when we arrive.

'That's odd,' says Mum. 'We did let them know we were coming. We want to source some good chocolate for our new episode.'

'Maybe it's a mistake,' says Dad. 'We'll soon find out.' He pushes his hair out of his eyes. His fringe is always flopping in the way of his face – except when he tucks it under his cap for cooking.

We trudge across a pebbly car park, Mum clutching her clipboard.

I snap a picture of the outside of the factory and quickly send it to Lucy.

We're here. Not sure there's anyone inside though. Shame, I was looking forward to the chocolate.

The door is ajar. Perhaps the sign was a mistake and they really are open. As Dad pushes it open a heavenly smell tickles my nostrils. Chocolate! Only the best food in the whole world.

Mum and Dad smell it too, and we stand taking deep breaths, looking around at the shelves and tables piled high with chocolate. There are cardboard-wrapped bars, cellophane packets and elaborate-looking boxes covering every surface. On the far side of the shop a refrigerated counter display holds single chocolates. I can't wait to get closer and see what they're like.

A voice from across the shop startles us.

'What do you want? Can't you see we are closed?'

An angry face appears above the counter. A lady with spiky black hair, bright red lipstick and big dangly earrings points at the door as she speaks.

She moves out from behind the counter and I see she is wearing a black-and-white outfit – checked pants and a white shirt, with a big black apron. The apron has telltale brown smudges that say she has been making chocolate.

Mum holds out her hand. 'I'm not sure you understand. We have an appointment. We are the Cooksons, from the show –'

'Oh.' The lady arches an eyebrow. A look I don't quite understand crosses her face. Is it a scowl? 'You're the Cooksons?' she says, as if she doesn't believe it. She looks at Mum and Dad, then at me.

'Yes,' says Dad. 'I'm Basil, and this is my wife Ginger.'

The strange woman doesn't smirk like people sometimes do when they hear my parents' names, but she does look at me with cold, dark eyes.

'And this is our daughter Sage,' Mum says, introducing me. Again, no smirk. I guess she might already know about our flavourful names.

The woman swallows before she speaks, then smiles a small smile. 'Of course you're the Cooksons. You must forgive my rudeness.' She wipes her hands on her apron before reaching out to shake our hands. 'It's an honour to have you here. A real honour.'

Mum smiles. She's used to people being excited about meeting her and Dad.

It makes some people nervous, because they're famous. I find it funny, because to me they're just Mum and Dad.

'Well you might know who we are, but may I ask your name?'

The woman frowns. 'Oh I'm so sorry.' She doesn't look very sorry. 'How rude of me. I'm Nancy. I am Marco's assistant.'

Dad offers his hand. 'It's nice to meet you, Nancy. We are here to talk to Marco. Is he expecting us? We did notice the closed sign, and wondered –'

Nancy cuts Dad off. 'Oh no!' she says. 'Of course we have been waiting for you. We just closed for the day so nobody would interrupt us.' She looks behind Mum and Dad. 'And you are alone? Just the three of you?'

Mum smiles. 'Yes. We didn't bring the film crew. I thought perhaps today we could have a chat and see what you do, and then, if it suits, come back later in the week for some filming?'

The woman frowns again, just briefly, before smiling. 'Well, we'll see what Marco says about that, shall we?'

It is my turn to frown. Does she think Marco won't want to be filmed? Usually people are delighted to be part of the show. It helps make their own products more famous.

As we follow Nancy towards the back of the store my phone vibrates silently in my pocket.

I quickly check it.

We won netball. Hope you find that chocolate.

I smile to myself as I hurry to catch up with the others. My reply to Lucy will have to wait.

CHAPTER 5

We go through a door marked *Staff Only*. Oddly, as soon as we're through, Nancy slides a lock behind us. Is she locking us in, I wonder, or keeping intruders out?

'Marco,' Nancy calls. 'The Cooksons are here.' Again I see a funny look cross her face. Almost a look of distaste, like she's swallowed something bad. My parents don't seem to notice.

Marco comes from behind a counter on

the other side of a big kitchen. He is a small, dark-haired man, wearing a uniform just like Nancy's, though less smeared and more neatly arranged. He claps his hands together as Nancy ushers us into the kitchen.

'Ah. The Cooksons! How lovely! Welcome to my humble chocolaterie!' He smiles, though like Nancy the smile doesn't seem to go all the way to his eyes. I can't help thinking that something is wrong. He shakes hands with Mum and Dad, then turns to me. 'Now I know who these two are –' He gestures at Mum and Dad. 'But you, beautiful young lady, you I don't know.' He offers his hand.

I feel myself blush. I'm not used to strangers telling me I'm beautiful. 'I'm Sage.' I shake his hand. 'Sage Cookson.'

'Ah. So there are not two Cooksons but three?' He smiles, and I wonder if I imagined the tension a few moments before. 'These two are the ones on the TV – so you, I'm guessing, must be their assistant.' He gives me a wink. 'I'll bet you're the chief chocolate taster?'

I laugh. 'How did you guess?' I know he's joking, but I'm also pretty keen to taste as much chocolate as I can.

Marco gives us a tour of the factory.

In the kitchen area we see the big vats where the chocolate is mixed. One vat is clean and empty, but the other is moving, stirring a huge batch of shiny brown chocolate.

The smell of warm chocolate makes my mouth water.

'These are the moulds for this batch.' Marco shows us a set of plastic trays divided into dozens of smaller sections. He turns to Nancy. 'This lot is almost ready for pouring. Make sure you don't let it spoil.'

Leaving Nancy to work, Marco takes us to see the storeroom full of cocoa and other ingredients. Again, the smell of cocoa and butter and sugar and sweet heaven is almost too much to bear. I just want to eat something! At last he takes us back through to the showroom.

'This is where our customers come. They don't get the same tour as you.'

I look around, again noting all the wrapped chocolate in all sorts of packages. A small display against one wall shows how chocolate is made.

Marco shows me a big seed pod. 'Do you know what this is?'

I shake my head. It's not like any seed I've seen before.

'It is cocoa! This is the seed from which comes the flavour in all these chocolates.' His hand sweeps the room. 'We source the best cocoa from around the world – Brazil, Ghana, Mexico, even sometimes Papua New Guinea. Each region produces its own distinct taste.'

'Really?' Dad asks. 'So you can tell the different tastes?'

'Oh, but of course. Come and see.' Marco leads us to a tasting table. 'Our finest chocolates are our single-source chocolates. These are each made with the cocoa from a single place.'

He slices thin slivers of three different chocolates. At last, I'm getting to taste the chocolate!

Marco is right. The chocolate piece from Brazil has a different taste to the one from Ghana. It's a subtle difference but it's there.

'This one tastes almost nutty,' I say.

Marco claps his hand together. 'Perfect! That is exactly right.' He beams. 'See, I knew you were the chocolate taster. Some people say they can't taste the difference. But a connoisseur like you can tell.'

As we head back towards the kitchen I manage a quick text to Lucy.

Found the chocolate. It's divine. Will definitely be bringing some back to share.

I sense someone looking at me as I follow my parents and Marco. I glance back and see Nancy watching us. Marco might be smiling, but Nancy most definitely isn't. I wonder what is wrong with her.

CHAPTER 6

'Now, I have a surprise for you,' Marco says, rubbing his hands together. 'I have my own supply of cocoa, growing near here.'

It is Dad's turn to frown. 'Here? Isn't it too cold this far south?'

I think Dad's right. I remember reading somewhere that cocoa usually grows in tropical places.

But Marco's eyes are full of steel. 'Do you think I would lie?' All traces of the smiling, smooth-talking host of a few minutes before is gone.

Mum nudges Dad and talks quickly. 'Of course not! We've just never heard of cocoa being grown in this part of the world before.'

Marco smiles thinly. 'Haven't you? Well, perhaps that's because it is a secret I have kept. A special new variety of cocoa. Can I trust you not to spread the word on your program?'

The look he gives us is almost menacing. A shiver runs down my spine. It's as if the sun has slipped behind a cloud. Mum and Dad don't seem to notice, quickly reassuring Marco that they can be trusted.

'It's always an honour to see something groundbreaking,' Mum says. 'Of course we can keep it confidential.'

'You'd bett– ' Marco begins, then stops himself. 'Er – of course it is an honour to be showing my work to such famous chefs as the Cooksons.' He looks at me. 'And their beautiful daughter, of course.' This time I don't feel pleased to be called beautiful. Marco is starting to creep me out. One moment he's smiling and welcoming, the next he's moody and confusing. I don't trust him.

Mum and Dad are quiet too, but we get into Marco's dual cab truck and pull away from the building.

Through the window I see Nancy watching us drive away. Her smile suggests she's happy to see us leave.

In the back seat I text Lucy.

Off to look at some cocoa trees. Didn't know they grew here.

Lucy replies quickly. My phone is on silent but I feel it vibrate and glance down at the screen.

You sure? I thought cocoa was a tropical plant.

I'm about to reply when Mum, who's in the back with me, looks over.

'Put it away, Sage,' she says. 'Just enjoy the view.'

I slip the phone into my pocket. I can answer Lucy later.

Mum is right: the drive is beautiful, though the road is fairly bumpy as we head deep into the bush. Tall trees tower over the car in the valleys, then we climb up hills with smaller trees and lots of scrub.

In the front, Dad tries to make conversation with Marco.

'How big is your cocoa plantation?' he asks.

'Big enough,' grunts Marco. He is concentrating on the road, which has narrowed until it is just a track.

'Is it hard to grow out here?' Dad asks.

Marco grunts again. 'No.'

Dad looks puzzled. He is used to fellow food lovers wanting to share their passions. He tries again.

'So, how long has it taken –'

'What's with the questions?' Marco snaps. 'Don't you trust me or something?'

Dad is quiet after that. I see him chewing his bottom lip, something he does when he is worried. Something is wrong here. I feel it and Dad feels it too. I glance across at Mum who seems to be still enjoying the view, but when I look closely even she looks worried. She twists a strand of hair around one finger, releases it, then does it again.

I don't know how long we drive for, but it seems like hours. We go further and further into the bush, and the scenery seems to grow darker and wilder. We head down into a gully where the trees are high and the ground below shaded. Wild vines grow everywhere, and the warm day is blocked out. I shiver, and I'm not sure whether it's because it is getting cold or because I'm scared. Something is *definitely* wrong.

'Marco, I think –' Dad starts.

'Be quiet, will you!' Marcus snaps. 'I'm in charge here.'

Now I'm really frightened. I look at Mum and her face is white, though when she sees me looking she tries to give me a reassuring smile. She reaches over and pats my hand.

Finally, Marco stops the car.

'Get out,' he says. I notice that his accent has disappeared. Before he sounded French. Now I'm not so sure.

Mum and Dad climb out of the car slowly, anxiously looking at their surroundings. I follow, taking a quick look at my phone when I hope nobody can see me. There is no signal, so no point trying to text Lucy now. Still, I push the phone into my pocket, hoping maybe a signal will pop up soon. I have a feeling we may need it.

CHAPTER 7

'So, Marco,' Mum licks her lips, something else she does when she's nervous. 'Where's the cocoa growing?'

She looks at the trees around us as if hoping one of them will suddenly turn into a cocoa tree. I have to admit I'm not sure what a cocoa tree looks like, but I can't see anything that looks like it was planted here by Marco. This is bush, filled with tall ancient trees, low shrubs and grasses.

Marco laughs. 'Cocoa, schmoko!' He claps his hands together. 'You fools. You are so busy thinking you have some kind of coup for your silly little cooking show that you will believe anything I tell you. Cocoa in the Australian bush? Ha!' He laughs again.

My parents don't look surprised, but they do look worried. They glance at each other for a moment before Dad finally speaks.

'I don't get it. You lie to us about having cocoa and then you drive us out into the bush. What's your point?'

'My point,' says Marco, who is walking backwards in the direction of his car, 'is simple. I brought you out here to leave you here.' He pulls a piece of paper from his top pocket and thrusts it towards Mum. 'You aren't in town to film for your silly little show. You want to win this! Well too bad! I plan to win with my chocolate mousse concoction. I won last year and I will win again. If you are stuck out here, then you can't win!'

Mum takes the piece of paper, looking confused, but Dad rushes towards the truck.

He's too late.

Marco has jumped into the driver's seat and starts the engine. I hear the ominous thunk of the locks as he latches the doors.

There's nothing we can do, though Dad bangs on the side of the truck in frustration. With a spin of the wheels, Marco turns and drives away as fast as he can.

'Come back! Stop!' we call after him, but of course he doesn't.

Together the three of us stand watching the truck disappear. A cloud of dust billows around the vehicle. We watch Marco almost hit a tree as the truck's wheels slip in the loose gravel.

We look at each other in disbelief. Is he really abandoning us?

CHAPTER 8

Mum is still clutching the piece of paper Marco thrust at her. She unfolds it, reads it and gives a kind of laugh.

'You're joking!' she says, passing the paper to Dad.

'Idiot!' Dad says as he reads it, but he too looks like he's almost smiling.

I don't get the joke, and hold my hand out for the piece of paper.

I read it.

10TH ANNUAL
NEWHAVEN COOKING CONTEST

BIG PRIZES ON OFFER FOR BEST:

MAIN COURSE
PASTRY DISH
DESSERT ... AND MORE

GRAB AN ENTRY FORM AND GET COOKING BECAUSE
THIS YEAR THE PRIZES ARE BIGGER

AND THE GUEST JUDGES ARE A FABULOUS SURPRISE!

'I don't see what's funny,' I say.

Mum giggles. I can tell she's still stressed, but even at a time like this her sense of humour is obvious.

'Marco is so determined to win the

cooking contest that he has just stranded the guest judges in the middle of the bush!'

'Guest judges?' I read the invitation again, then look at Mum and Dad. 'You two are the guest judges?' I shake my head. 'But why didn't you tell him?

'He didn't give us a chance, did he?' says Dad. 'Besides which, it's supposed to be a secret. We're even going to film some of the judging for the show.'

He strokes his jaw, thinking. 'But it seems Marco got the wrong end of the stick, and thought we were in town so we could enter the contest for ourselves.'

'And now,' says Mum, looking around, as if she's forgotten for a moment where we are, 'he's left us out here. There won't be any judges if we don't figure out a way to get back.'

I look at the track that Marco brought us

down. It goes back up the gully, then twists out of sight behind towering trees and massive boulders. It had been sunny when we left the chocolate factory, but above us the trees block out much of the light.

'What are we going to do?' I ask.

'Isn't much we can do,' says Dad. 'Guess we'd better start walking.'

'Could we ring for help?' Mum asks, looking around as she remembers something. 'Drat! My bag is still in Marco's car. It's got all my notes for the series, my hotel keys – and my phone.'

'Mine too,' said Dad. 'I left it in the centre console.'

I reach into my pocket. 'Ta da!' I say, holding mine up. 'Guess you're glad you got me this then?' I look hopefully at the screen for a moment and feel my smile fade. 'But there's no signal.'

Mum kicks a rock and it skitters away into the bush.

Dad says something he shouldn't, then takes a deep breath. 'Guess we're walking then.'

CHAPTER 9

'Something beginning with, um ...'
Dad looks around wearily. We've
been playing I Spy for an hour
now as we trudge along the track. 'C,' he
says finally.

'Chocolate,' I answer, without really
stopping to think.

'Not too much of that out here,' Mum
says. 'Wish we'd tried some more samples
from the factory while we had the chance.'

My mouth waters at the thought of all

that chocolatey goodness we saw, smelled and tasted only this morning. I can't help wondering if we'll ever get to taste chocolate again.

We've been walking for hours, trudging along the track, hoping that it's the same one we travelled on with Marco earlier in the day. From time to time we find other tracks leading off into the bush, and none of us is really sure that we are on the right one. We just keep hoping.

We're also hoping that sooner or later I'll get a signal on my mobile phone and we can call for help. I look at the darkening sky. If we don't get help soon we are going to be out in the bush all night.

'Aren't you guys going to guess?' asks Dad. It takes me a moment to remember the game.

Dad is smiling, though.

'Give up?' He hardly waits for us to answer. 'It's a camp site. Over there!'

And he's right. Just ahead of us, a smaller track branches off the one we are walking on and heads down a slope into a camping area. There are no campers, but there are concrete picnic tables, two fireplaces and, at the far side of the clearing, an old toilet.

Mum and I both make a quick dash for that, obviously thinking the same thing. We ignore the spiders and cobwebs in the dim cubicle, grateful just for the relief.

Back in the clearing, we all sit at one of the concrete tables, glad to have a place to rest. There is no sign of any other campers – and if the cobwebs in the toilet are anything to go by, it's been a while since anyone else was here – but still, a camp site is a sign of civilisation, and our spirits lift just a little bit.

'We are getting closer,' says Mum. 'I'm sure we'll get help soon.'

Right on cue, something beeps in my pocket.

'My phone!' I pull it out. 'We must have a signal here.'

There is a text from Lucy.

How's it going? Did you find the cocoa trees? I checked online and couldn't find anything about cocoa growing that far south.

No time to tell her she's right. I have to get help. I hit reply.

Help! We're stuck in the bush. Marco abandoned us.

'What are you doing?' says Mum. 'Don't waste time texting. We need to phone the police.'

I hit send anyway, then pass the phone to her outstretched hand. She's right. A phone call is probably quicker.

Mum punches some numbers into the keypad and holds the phone to her ear, smiling slightly. I watch her face, waiting anxiously to see how quickly help will be on its way.

Next to me, Dad taps his fingers on the table.

'Hello?' Mum's smile grows. There must be a voice on the other end. 'I –' She stops. 'Hello? Hello?' She pulls the phone away from her ear, frowning at the screen. 'Oh no!' Her smile disappears. 'We lost the signal!'

I peer at the screen, hoping she's wrong. But she's not.

CHAPTER 10

Dad grabs the phone from Mum and holds it above his head, trying to get a signal. He climbs a tree, waving the phone in the air, but it doesn't happen anyway.

Mum takes it back and walks out into the clearing. 'Maybe the trees are interfering,' she says. But I can see from the look on her face that the signal isn't coming back.

She passes the phone back to me and I try to figure out exactly where I was standing when it beeped, and what position I was holding it in. If I had a signal there a minute ago, surely I can get it back.

'No luck?' Mum asks, even though she must guess the answer. I shake my head, blinking back the tears of frustration and fear that fill my eyes.

'I suppose we'd better keep walking then,' says Dad miserably. 'Let's hope we're heading the right way.'

As we cast final longing looks at the camp site, a shadow falls across us. Peering up through the trees, I see dark clouds rolling across the sky. It's late afternoon, so it will be dark soon – and the presence of clouds means we could be in for a wet night too.

'Wait,' I say to Mum and Dad. 'Are you sure we should keep walking?' I point up at the sky. 'It's getting late and it looks like it might even rain. Maybe we should stay where we are, try to shelter until help comes.'

Dad looks uncertain, but Mum shakes her head sadly. 'I'm not sure help will come, sweetheart. Nobody knows we're here.'

'Nobody except Marco,' Dad growls.

'And Nancy,' I say, remembering the look on her face this morning. 'But I don't think she's going to come and rescue us.' I think for a moment. 'What about Sheila and Dave?'

Dad shrugs. 'They'll notice we're not there, of course, but they won't know where to look for us. Probably won't even get worried till bedtime. Might think we've gone out to dinner, or found a great location or something.'

He's right. It's not unusual for them to spend whole days away from the crew, especially when we first arrive in a new place. Often Mum and Dad (and me, if I'm there) will go and check out some places, while Dave and Sheila check out others, to save time. Today they were supposed to be visiting the local wineries to find some great filming locations.

'But they'll miss us eventually, surely?' I ask.

Dad nods. 'Of course, but not till after dark. Maybe not even until morning.'

I can feel tears threatening again, and blink to clear them. I have to trust that everything is going to be okay.

'You know what,' says Mum, 'you might be right, Sage. There is shelter here, a place to sit –'

'And a toilet,' I remind her. Neither of us is keen on peeing behind trees, even out here where nobody can see us.

Her little smile is back. "So maybe we should rest here overnight then head off as soon as it gets light.'

Dad finally agrees, and we set about trying to figure out how to make the camp site more comfortable.

I bend close to the ash-filled fireplaces, hoping against hope that there might be a single warm coal or ember that we can use to get a new fire started to keep warm. No such luck, but Mum and Dad have started searching for big leafy branches, which they drag over to one of the tables. By leaning them against the sides they create a kind of three-walled cave so we'll be able to sit under the table if we get too cold.

We consider the toilet briefly, in spite of being grossed out at the thought of sleeping near it, but the walls are made of rusting tin and don't go all the way to the ground. When someone is in there, you can see their feet.

'Besides,' says Dad, 'I don't like the look of that big branch hanging low over the roof.

Looks like it could drop at any time.'

So a nest under the camp table it is.

At first we sit or lie on the benches, chatting about whatever we can think of to take our minds off our predicament, but after the sun goes down it gets colder and colder, and rain starts falling. We huddle under the table, grateful for the warmth we can give each other. We try hard to stay dry, but the shelter is small and open on one side, and we can feel the damp spreading through our clothes.

Worse than that, though, is the croaking. As soon as the rain starts, the frogs start singing their spooky song. *Croak croak croak.* Every time something moves nearby, I am sure a frog is going to jump on me. Gross!

'Don't be silly,' says Mum, when I tell her my fears. 'The frogs are just happy to have some moisture to move around in. They're not interested in you.'

'What do you think they'll do?' asks Dad. 'Slap you with their long tongues?'

'Daaaaad,' I say, horrified at the very thought of being licked by a frog. I just do not like frogs *at all*. I'd rather see a spider or maybe even a snake than a green, slimy, spooky frog.

It is a long, long night, and none of us really sleep, although I doze off a few times and at one point Dad must too because he lets out one big snore then sits up, startled. It would be funny if we weren't hiding under a table in the middle of nowhere.

CHAPTER 11

Beep.

A strange noise wakes me from a troubled sleep. I blink, momentarily not sure where I am. Then I remember. I'm cramped under a table with Mum and Dad. Outside there is cold rain drip-dripping from the trees. And the frogs are still croak-oaking.

Beep. My phone! We must have a signal again.

Crawling out from under the table, I grab

the phone out of my pocket and press the button. The screen lights up and I see I have a stack of missed messages.

Where are you? Call me!

You okay? Tell me what's happening.

You missed a call from Lucy Trent, who did not leave a message.

'Mum! Dad! My phone's working again.' Now my parents crawl out from under the table too, blinking in the early morning light. Dad grabs the phone from me.

'Great, now we can phone for help.'

He opens the keypad and starts to press numbers, then stops. 'Noooooooooo!' He grunts in frustration. 'You have got to be kidding me!'

'What is it?' Mum frowns. 'Did you lose the signal again?'

'I think the battery's flat,' says Dad, shaking the phone as if that might make it work again.

We look at each other in disbelief. We are wet, we are cold, we are hungry and tired, and our lifeline has just died.

'Let's walk,' Mum finally mumbles.

Through the dim morning light we follow the track that we hope will take us back to Newhaven. We try to cheer each other up with reassurances that we must be almost there, but none of us is sure that that's true.

We trudge trudge trudge along the track. It is wet and slippery in some places and just plain squelchy in others. The rain is still dripping down, though it's hard to tell if it's coming from the sky, or if the rain has stopped above the canopy and the drips are just coming from the wet leaves above us. Either way, we are wet and miserable.

I can still hear frogs, and another sound now – the whine of mosquitoes. Happy to have some fresh human blood to suck,

I guess, they swarm around us, and as we walk we brush and swat at them.

I think of Lucy telling me to have a brilliant time – was that only two days ago?

'Oh yes,' I mutter. 'Really brilliant!'

'What was that, honey?' asks Mum.

'Nothing,' I say. 'Talking to myself really.' I know there's no point complaining. Mum and Dad are just as uncomfortable and dejected as I am.

'Check your phone again,' says Dad. 'Maybe it's working now.'

I sigh, shaking my head. There's no point, but I pull the phone from my pocket anyway. Nothing. The screen is still dark.

We trudge some more, so lost in our miserableness that we don't notice the changes about us. It takes me a while, but then I realise three things: there is sunshine starting to warm me, the frogs have got quieter, and there's another noise. Something different. Something –

'A car!' I cry. 'I can hear a car!'

'Are you sure?' says Dad, and we stop and listen.

There's the noise again. It's the unmistakable sound of a motor somewhere, and it's getting closer.

We smile and start running along the track, hoping that we are heading towards the sound. In the bush, it's hard to be sure.

We round a bend and can't believe our eyes. A white four-wheel drive is coming towards us, a yellow flashing light spinning on its roof.

'Over here!' we call, not stopping to think that the driver won't hear us over the sound of the engine. We jump up and down, waving our arms.

'Thank goodness!' says Dad as the vehicle

comes to a stop. He throws one arm around my shoulder and the other around Mum's as we hurry over. We're all smiling, and our tiredness of a few moments ago has disappeared.

The driver's door opens and a man gets out. He's wearing a khaki uniform and has a big smile on his face.

'The Cooksons, I presume?'

We just nod enthusiastically.

'Just a minute,' he says, and takes a two-way radio off his belt. 'I've found them,' he says. The voice on the other end says something I can't quite make out. 'They look fine,' he says. 'A bit wet, but not injured. I'll bring them back in.'

He puts the radio away.

'Sorry about that,' he says. 'Just had to let base know you were okay. I'm Tom,' he says, offering his hand.

'Ginger,' says Mum. 'And this is Basil, my husband, and Sage, our daughter.' She smiles. 'And we are very very glad to meet you, Tom.'

'I'll bet you are,' says Tom. 'We'd have come looking for you sooner but only heard that you might be out here an hour ago.' He explains that Lucy got my text but wasn't sure how serious it was. Finally, her parents had managed to contact Sheila, who had raised the alarm.

'But how did you know where to look for us?'

Tom looks uncomfortable. 'I'm not sure I'm supposed to say,' he says, 'but a lady called Nancy had some information that the police thought was helpful. Anyway, hop in and I'll get you back to town.' He hands us each a water bottle, which we slurp at keenly.

Mum and I settle in to the back seat, and Dad climbs in the front. I sit close to Mum, and soon my head is on her shoulder. I doze most of the way back into town, which Tom says is about twenty kilometres away. Just as well we didn't have to walk the whole way.

CHAPTER 12

*W*e are safe and back in the hotel. *Thanks for raising the alarm. Will ring you as soon as my phone finishes charging.*

I leave the phone on the charger and climb into the hot bubble bath that Sheila has just run for me. I'm staying at the hotel with Sheila and Dave while Mum and Dad make a report at the police station.

The bath water is lovely. Steam rises around me and the lavender-scented bubbles are heavenly. I rest my head on the edge and lie back. My eyes start to close.

'Don't fall asleep in there,' Sheila's voice warns through the door, at just the right moment.

'I won't,' I call back, not telling her that I nearly did just that.

'Dave's going to organise some food. Is there anything you want especially?'

'No,' I reply. 'Just something yummy.' My stomach rumbles at the mention of food. 'And lots of it.'

I hear Sheila chuckle before she starts talking to Dave.

I smile to myself, thinking how scary last night was, and how great it is to be back in the hotel. I'm still a bit hazy on how we came to be rescued, but I'm pretty happy to be here.

After my bath, I wrap myself in the fluffy

bathrobe the hotel has supplied. Out in my room, Sheila has set up a tray for me on the table looking out over the view.

'Come and eat,' she says. 'And tell me what happened.'

I tuck into the delicious food: steaming chicken soup with crusty bread, and a strawberry sundae for dessert.

I tell her about meeting Marco and Nancy, the drive into the bush and our horror at being left behind. Then I tell her about the long night cramped under the table, and the croaking of the frogs, as I finish off my sundae.

'They are horrible!' I say. 'Slimy, noisy, and –'

Sheila frowns. 'I guess you won't be wanting these, then?'

She has a small paper bag next to her chair.

'What are they?' I ask.

She laughs as she hands the bag to me. 'I just wasn't thinking,' she says.

I have to giggle when I open it. 'Frogs!' Two delicious-looking chocolate frogs nestle in the bag.

'I thought you might want a chocolate fix.' She looks sheepish. 'I didn't think about the fact that I was combining the two things from your little adventure – chocolate and frogs.'

I laugh. 'That's okay,' I say, nibbling one of the delicious chocolates. 'These are the only frogs I like. And *nothing* will ever turn me off chocolate.'

CHAPTER 13

'Good afternoon everybody, and welcome to the awards ceremony for the tenth annual Newhaven Cooking Contest.'

Standing at the back of the room, I clap along with the rest of the gathered crowd. It's our last day in Newhaven, and Mum and Dad are about to announce the winners of the cooking competition. Sheila and Dave are busy filming everything.

'First up,' the master of ceremonies is

saying, 'I would like to introduce our special judges, who have had a hard time judging all of the delicacies you provided for them.' He pauses for a moment. 'But perhaps not as difficult a time as they had earlier in the week.' There is a buzz around the room. People have probably guessed that it's Mum and Dad. Word about our adventures seems to have spread pretty quickly.

'From the television sensation *The Cooksons Cook On* – it's Ginger and Basil Cookson!'

The room erupts in applause as Mum and Dad appear on the stage.

'Thank you,' says Mum. 'It's an honour to be invited to Newhaven. We have really had a lovel– ' She pauses. 'Er, an *interesting* time here.' There is a ripple of uncomfortable laughter. 'But we promise you, we bear no ill feeling towards your town. We will be taking away lots of wonderful memories.'

The crowd claps, and I can see some people look relieved. Mum had told me that the business owners were worried that Mum and Dad might talk about their terrible experience and then tourists might not want to visit Newhaven.

Mum goes on. 'Now, to the winners of the contest.'

There are plenty of oohs and aahs as the delicious concoctions are brought out on stage. There are steaming dishes of chicken and beef, pastry creations sprinkled with sugar, and a chocolate mousse that I am sure tastes as good as anything Marco could have made.

When Mum and Dad present the final prize, the room fills with applause and smiles and good feelings. I smile, too. We're safe and Marco is in jail, at least until his court appearance. We've had a lovely few days exploring, sampling good food and filming.

My phone, which is on silent in my pocket, buzzes. I know the message will be from Lucy, and I smile again as I tap my pocket. I'm not allowed to use my phone during the speeches, but they'll be over soon, and then I can send a reply.

Coming home tomorrow and bringing chocolate.

Marco and Nancy have not managed to ruin my love for chocolate, and they sure won't have ruined Lucy's.

I look up, and someone standing near the door startles me. Leaning against the doorframe, watching the awards with a face like thunder, is someone I had hoped never to see again. 'Nancy!' I whisper to myself, my stomach clenching. I can't believe she has come here after what Marco did to us.

Nancy sees me looking and slips away. *Good riddance*, I think. Dad has explained that, although the police have arrested and charged Marco, they had no choice but to let Nancy free. She insisted she didn't know what Marco was planning, and she did give the police some ideas about where to look when Lucy raised the alarm. If she hadn't have done that, we might not have been found.

A shiver runs down my spine at the thought.

'What's the matter, Sage?' Mum is standing beside me. The presentations have finished without me noticing.

I smile. 'Nothing,' I say.

'Good. Then let's go home,' she says.

'Yes, let's.' I don't tell her about seeing Nancy. We're leaving now, flying back home to the other side of the country.

I send that text to Lucy. I can't wait to see her again tomorrow.

ABOUT THE AUTHOR

Sally Murphy is a mum, wife, daughter, teacher, speaker, website manager, reviewer, storyteller, PhD candidate and, of course, author. While that sounds like a lot of things to be at once, she still finds time to play with her kids, read books, watch TV, cook, clean and a million other things. She thrives on being busy and, when she sees a gap, she quickly plugs it with another project.

Delicious chocolate pudding

Vanilla ice cream

Gooey chocolate centre

CHEAT'S CHOCOLATE FONDANT

Serves 6

140g softened butter

250g caster sugar

2 eggs

300g (2 cups) plain flour

1 teaspoon baking powder

60g cocoa

265ml milk

1 small jar (220g) of chocolate spread

Preheat the oven to 170°C.

Grease six small ramekins with butter.

Beat the butter and sugar until pale and creamy. Add the eggs and beat to combine. Sift the flour, baking powder and cocoa over the butter mixture and stir to combine. Stir in milk.

Spoon one large tablespoon of batter into each of the ramekins, add a tablespoon of Nutella to the centre of each and spoon over the rest of the batter, dividing it evenly between the six ramekins.

Bake for approximately 12–15 minutes, until the tops crack and a skewer comes out of the pudding clean. (Remember the chocolate spread centre and avoid it with the skewer).

Serve warm with vanilla ice-cream.